POPPLETON
Forever

CYNTHIA RYLANT

POPPLETON
Forever

BOOK FOUR

Illustrated by
MARK TEAGUE

SCHOLASTIC INC.
New York Toronto London Auckland Sydney

To Mark and Emily
M. T.

This book is being published simultaneously in hardcover by the Blue Sky Press.

ISBN 0-590-84844-5

Text copyright © 1998 by Cynthia Rylant
Illustrations copyright © 1998 by Mark Teague
All rights reserved. Published by Scholastic Inc.

SCHOLASTIC and associated logos are trademarks and/or registered trademarks of Scholastic Inc.

20 19 18 17 16 15   11 12 13/0

Printed in the United States of America   40

Design by Kathleen Westray

First Scholastic paperback printing, August 1998

CONTENTS

THE TREE

Poppleton planted a new little tree
in his yard.
It was a dogwood.
Poppleton liked it very much.

He watered it every day.

He gave it tree food.

He staked it against the wind.

The little tree grew strong and fast.

Poppleton was pleased.

Then one day the tree looked awful.

Its leaves drooped.

Its bark peeled.

It turned from green to brown.

"Oh no!" said Poppleton,

when he saw his tree.

He called the tree doctor.

"Come right away!" said Poppleton.

The tree doctor came

to look at Poppleton's tree.

He tapped it.

He stroked it.

He felt its trunk and leaves.

The tree doctor said to Poppleton,

"This tree needs something,

but I don't know what it is."

"Can't you just give it a pill?"
asked Poppleton.
"It isn't sick," said the tree doctor.
"It *needs* something."
Poppleton did not know
what his little tree needed.

He tapped it.

He stroked it.

He felt its trunk and leaves.

But he did not know.

Poppleton sat up with his tree all night,
wondering what it needed.

In the morning he went for help.

"What does my tree need?" Poppleton

asked Hudson down the street.

"A piece of cheese?" said Hudson.

Poppleton gave the tree a piece
of cheese, but it didn't help.

"What does my tree need?" Poppleton
asked Newhouse, the delivery dog.
"A bone?" said Newhouse.

Poppleton gave the tree a bone,
but it didn't help.

Poppleton went to see Cherry Sue.

"What does my tree need?"
Poppleton asked Cherry Sue.
Cherry Sue looked out her window
at the little tree.
She thought and thought.

Then she said, "If I were that tree,
I would need a bird feeder."
"A bird feeder?" asked Poppleton.
"Trees want birds," said Cherry Sue.
"Why do you think they hold out
their arms all day?"

Poppleton bought a bird feeder
for his little tree.

A sparrow came,
and a leaf turned green.

A cardinal came,
and another leaf turned green.

A bluebird came,
and three leaves turned green.

Poppleton's tree got better.

Soon all of its leaves were green.

"You are a pretty smart llama,"
Poppleton told Cherry Sue.
"You are a pretty nice pig,"
Cherry Sue told him.
Then they had lemonade
and watched the birds.

THE COLD

Poppleton had an awful cold.

He sneezed and sneezed.

Tissues were all over his house.

His neighbor Cherry Sue
knocked on his door.
She had a bowl full of ten oranges.
"Oranges are good for colds,
Poppleton," said Cherry Sue.

Poppleton nodded his head.

He was too stuffy to talk.

Cherry Sue went home, and

Poppleton peeled an orange.

AH-CHOOOOOO!

The orange flew out of Poppleton's
hands and landed in the fish tank.
Poppleton peeled another orange.

AH-CHOOOOOO!

The orange flew out of Poppleton's
hands and landed in the piano.
Poppleton peeled a third orange.

AH-CHOOOOOO!

The orange flew out of Poppleton's hands
and landed in the washing machine.

Poppleton peeled one orange
after another and kept on sneezing.
Soon there were ten peeled oranges
in strange places all over his house.

Later Cherry Sue knocked
on Poppleton's door.
She had a bowl full of eggs.
"Eggs are good for colds, Poppleton,"
said Cherry Sue.
"Uh-oh," said Poppleton.

WALLPAPER

Poppleton bought some wallpaper
for his kitchen.
He asked his friend Hudson
to help him hang it.

"Sure," said Hudson.

Hudson came over
on Saturday morning.

Poppleton and Hudson put some glue
on the back of the wallpaper.
Then they tried to hang it on the wall.
"Hold up your side, Hudson,"
said Poppleton.

"I *am* holding up my side,"
said Hudson.

Poppleton looked over at Hudson.

Hmmm, thought Poppleton.
Maybe I shouldn't have asked a
three-inch mouse to help hang wallpaper.
"I'll call Fillmore to help us,"
said Poppleton.

Fillmore came over to help.

"Hold up your part, Fillmore,"
said Poppleton.

Poppleton looked over at Fillmore.

Fillmore was chewing on the paper.

Hmmm, thought Poppleton.
Maybe I shouldn't have asked a goat
to help hang wallpaper.
"I'll call Cherry Sue to help us,"
said Poppleton.

Cherry Sue came over to help.
"Hold up your part, Cherry Sue,"
said Poppleton.
Poppleton looked over at Cherry Sue.
Cherry Sue was stuck to the glue.

Hmmm, thought Poppleton.
*Maybe I shouldn't have asked a llama
to help hang wallpaper.*

"How can I hang wallpaper," Poppleton
complained to them all, "when Hudson
is a mouse, and Fillmore is a goat,
and Cherry Sue is a llama!"

The three friends looked at Poppleton.

"Oh dear," said Poppleton, ashamed.

"I can stand on a ladder," said Hudson.

"I can eat a big breakfast first,"
said Fillmore.

"I can get a haircut," said Cherry Sue.

Poppleton looked at his three dear friends.
Such good friends.
"And I can take you all out for ice cream!"
said Poppleton.

Which he did.

On their way back home, Poppleton
traded the wallpaper for some paint.

His friends were the finest painters
in town.